T☢XIC

" 'We're entering the atmosphere! Outside, the deep black of space had changed to a sky-blue colour.

'PREPARE FOR IMPACT!' shrieked Mr Graham. Five seconds later the craft hit the ground with a gigantic booming sound.

The next thing Jed knew was blackness. "

CRASH LAND EARTH

Crash Land Earth
by Jonny Zucker
Illustrated by Diego Diaz

Published by Ransom Publishing Ltd.
Radley House, 8 St. Cross Road, Winchester, Hampshire
SO23 9HX, UK
www.ransom.co.uk

ISBN   978 178127 714 0
First published in 2015

CRASH LAND EARTH

JONNY ZUCKER

ILLUSTRATED BY
DIEGO DIAZ

Ransom

CHAPTER 1

'WHAT'S HAPPENING?' yelled Jed, as the gleaming silver spaceship stopped for a moment and then suddenly started to nose-dive.

Mr Graham, Jed and the other three kids – Tariq, Jodie and Carla – were flung around like bullets, smashing into each other and against the walls.

'SEATBELTS! IMMEDIATELY!' barked Mr Graham.

The five of them were flung left and right, up and down, but they all managed to reach the seat harnesses and put them on.

Jed saw stars and dust clouds rush past the windows as the spaceship got faster and faster.

He couldn't believe it.

He was one of the first five people chosen to visit Mars, the famous *red planet*, and now their spaceship was going to crash, only seven days after take-off and millions of miles from their destination.

'WE'VE LOST THREE ENGINES!' shouted Mr Graham, pressing buttons and pulling levers desperately.

Jed felt an icy bolt of fear in his chest. The spaceship only had three engines! If they'd all gone, this mission and its passengers would be toast.

A piercing alarm started ringing every few seconds, its horrible electronic tone belting out its terrible news.

'WE'RE ALL GOING TO DIE!' screamed Tariq.

The ship tilted violently to the left, but the seatbelts held firm.

'ADOPT THE BRACE POSITION!' ordered Mr Graham, covering his head with his hands and arms.

The children immediately copied him. *We've been trained for this kind of emergency*, thought Jed. *But I never thought we'd need to use these skills.*

The ship was going incredibly fast and, as well as the noise of the alarm, it was now making a horrible high-pitched whistling sound, like a furious kettle.

'We're entering the atmosphere!' shouted Mr Graham.

Outside, the black of space had changed to a sky-blue colour.

Jed was pretty sure that Tariq was right. These were going to be his last few moments of life.

He thought about his parents and his little sister, Lilly. He'd never see them again. He'd never again hear Dad's crummy jokes, Mum's impressions of famous celebrities or Lilly's crazy singing.

'PREPARE FOR IMPACT!' shrieked Mr Graham.

Five seconds later, the craft hit the ground with a gigantic booming sound.

The next thing Jed knew was blackness.

CHAPTER 2

Jed opened his eyes slowly and winced as a pain on his forehead ripped through him.

Mr Graham and Jodie were leaning over him. Carla and Tariq were sitting on the floor, looking dazed.

'Just hold still a minute,' said Mr Graham, holding a piece of damp cloth against the large cut on Jed's forehead.

Jed winced in pain, but then Mr Graham covered the cut with a large bandage and the pain began to ease off.

'We are unbelievably lucky,' said Jodie, who had a giant purple bruise on her left cheek. 'We're all alive.'

'Jodie's right,' nodded Mr Graham.

'And we're doubly lucky,' murmured Tariq, slowly getting to his feet, 'because we've crash-landed on Earth.'

Jed looked out of the window and saw a hot, dusty desert stretching out around the spacecraft.

'It's remarkable,' nodded Mr Graham. 'We fell far further than I thought.'

'Can you radio the base?' asked Jed.

'Unfortunately all of our communications equipment was destroyed in the crash,' explained Mr Graham.

'And we have no idea where on Earth we are,' added Jodie. 'The GPS is wrecked as well.'

'But if we set out soon, we're bound to find someone who'll be able to help us,' said Mr Graham reassuringly.

*****

And so it was that, ten minutes later, the party of five stepped out of the smashed and battered spaceship.

The baking heat immediately hit them and, after choosing what Mr Graham felt was a northerly direction, they began their trek.

On the walk they passed a couple of large cactus plants and a few weary-looking trees.

The ship had been well stocked with provisions, so after a while they took a break and were all able to drink plenty of water and eat some energy supplies.

They got going again and, as Mr Graham predicted, an hour and a half later they climbed a steep hill and found themselves looking down at a small town.

'Brilliant!' cried Carla.

Jed was incredibly relieved. He'd imagined that they might have to walk for days, not hours, in the search for any signs of human life.

They walked down the other side of the hill, passed a large red-brick building and saw in the distance a young boy and girl who were throwing a ball to each other in a concrete yard.

Their movements were slightly stiff and jerky, which puzzled Jed, but Mr Graham was already heading straight for them.

'Hi you two,' he smiled warmly. 'We're new in town and we might need a bit of help getting home.'

The kids stared at Mr Graham and the four children standing behind him for a bit longer than was comfortable, but finally the boy said, 'You'll need to see the mayor. His office is in the centre of town.'

'Thanks,' replied Mr Graham, but the children said nothing.

They just ran away in that same jerky way that they'd been playing with the ball – as if their bodies had been made from ill-fitting pieces.

CHAPTER 3

On the road leading to the centre of town they passed a woman cutting a hedge and a man fixing a garage door.

They both nodded *hello*, but they also moved with the strange, clunky movements the ball-playing children had used.

The mayor's office was a large white building with highly polished windows and a large oak front door, which was open.

Mr Graham led the children inside.

The first thing they saw was a ruddy-cheeked man sitting behind a desk and gazing at a computer screen, with another, broader man with thin glasses standing beside him.

A large map of the town stood on the wall behind the mayor's desk. It showed the school, the hospital and somewhere called the 'Transport Hub', but the town itself didn't seem to have a name.

The two men smiled when Jed and the others entered.

'Glad you could all make it,' grinned the red-faced man, standing and shaking each of them by the hand. His handshakes weren't stiff at all.

'I'm the mayor, and this is our town medic, Dr Sark.'

The broad man nodded and he too shook their hands.

'So you've come to join the party?' enquired the mayor.

'Er … not quite,' said Jed, wondering what party they were talking about. 'We just want a bit of help to get back home. You see, we … '

'Of course you want to go home,' grinned the mayor. 'We all do. But we have to bide our time and strike when the moment is right.'

'I think there's been some kind of misunderstanding,' frowned Mr Graham. 'We're not here for a party. It's more transportation and direction we're looking for.'

'I completely understand,' replied the mayor. 'You'll find all of that stuff in the sports hall. Go take a look. You won't be disappointed!'

'Give them a break,' smiled Dr Sark kindly. 'They only just got here. Our mayor can be a bit over-enthusiastic sometimes, can't you?'

The mayor scowled but said nothing.

'OK … ' said Mr Graham slowly, 'we'll be on our way. Thanks for your help.'

*****

Once they were outside again, Mr Graham sighed. 'The mayor is a very strange man,' he declared, 'but that Dr Sark seems fine.'

Jed was only half-listening, as something about the mayor had attracted his attention.

It was a boiling-hot day and he, Mr Graham and the others were all sweating. The mayor, on the other hand, hadn't been sweating at all, even though his face had been very red and hot.

How could that be?

'The sports hall's over there,' said Tariq, pointing to a large green building across the road.

'Let's see what's going on,' nodded Mr Graham, but before any of them could take a single step, a huge steel bar about ten metres long came plummeting down from the sky, flying straight towards them.

CHAPTER 4

'MOVE!' screamed Mr Graham.

Everybody threw themselves backwards and the steel chunk buried itself in the ground, missing them by a couple of centimetres.

Tariq looked up. The steel had obviously fallen from a large crane that towered over them.

'WHAT DO YOU THINK YOU'RE DOING?' screeched Carla, shaking her fist at the guy driving the crane.

'What are you talking about?' he shot back. 'It wouldn't be a big deal if it had hit you, would it?'

'It's not funny!' snapped Jed. 'That steel would have killed us all!'

'Nice one,' laughed the driver. 'I'll make sure I hit you next time!'

He turned away and swung the grabber arm of the crane in another direction.

'I think we should go and check out the sports hall,' said Mr Graham, leading the

kids away from the mad-sense-of-humour
crane driver to the other side of the road.

*****

Entering the sports hall was a startling
experience. The place was enormous and
wherever you looked people were
participating in lightning-quick sports.

A large group of people were shinning up
and down high metal posts in ridiculously
fast times. A collection of teenagers were
involved in some kind of speeded-up
hand-to-hand combat. Some children and
adults were exchanging blows with long
metal bats.

It all looked very strange, but the
strangest part was that absolutely no one
seemed to be getting hurt. However far they
fell, however hard they were hit, they just

got back to their feet and launched straight into the action again.

'Do you want to sign up for anything?' asked a petite woman who blinked repeatedly.

'No thanks, we're fine,' said Tariq. 'We just like watching.'

'Watching is all well and good,' huffed the woman, 'but when the time comes and you really need some of these skills, you'll kick yourself that you didn't prepare properly.'

'Prepare for what?' asked Jodie in puzzlement.

'Hilarious,' muttered the woman sarcastically.

'We might sign up later,' said Mr Graham, 'but first we need to make our own preparations.'

'Fine,' nodded the woman curtly, 'we'll be expecting you back in a while.'

Mr Graham nodded at her and ushered the four teenagers to an exit door.

*****

They stepped back out into the sunshine and Mr Graham stroked his cheek as he thought about their current situation.

'This place is totally creeping me out,' said Jed. 'I say we make tracks and find another town.'

'I agree!' nodded Jodie. 'This place is full of weirdos.'

'I'll tell you what we'll do,' said Mr Graham. 'We'll go to that café over there, have a drink to cool down and then move on. What do you say?'

Everyone nodded, except for Jed.

'I've got a bad feeling about this place,' he said. 'I think we should head off right this second.'

CHAPTER 5

Jed was outvoted, and five minutes later they found themselves in the café.

It was dark inside, with red plastic chairs and white tables neatly laid out. A few customers nodded at them when they walked in, but most of the people ignored them.

The man serving at the counter was tall and slim, with some kind of red birthmark on his right cheek. He was smiling, but it was hard to know if it was a real smile or a fake one, as his face seemed permanently fixed in that expression.

Mr Graham took a seat at the counter and nodded to the others to do the same.

'Hi,' said Mr Graham. 'I was wondering if I could ask your advice?'

'Sure,' nodded the counter waiter with his fixed-on grin. 'How can I help you?'

'Well,' said Mr Graham, 'for starters, we aren't entirely sure where we are. So maybe you could help us with that one.'

'And we'd like to know where the next town is please,' said Jed. 'You know, somewhere a bit more normal.'

Mr Graham frowned at Jed, but the waiter didn't seem to mind this mini-insult at all.

'There's no need for you to go to another town,' replied the waiter. 'Everything you'll want or need is here. Besides, with so many others around you won't need to travel in isolation.'

For the first time, frustration sounded in Mr Graham's voice. His face tightened.

'Why does everyone speak like that in this place? Why can't anyone give a simple answer to a simple question?'

His voice had got louder and he was attracting attention.

'I'm just pointing out that soon we'll all be on the road together anyway,' said the

waiter, 'so there's no need to get all worked up about it, is there?'

Mr Graham shook his head wearily.

'OK,' he sighed. 'We'll have five of your coldest drinks, please.'

As soon as these words had come out of his mouth, the entire place went deathly silent.

'Did you just say … *cold* drinks?' asked the waiter slowly.

'Yes,' nodded Mr Graham. 'Any cold drinks will do. It's so hot around here.'

Suddenly, everyone in the café was on their feet. They no longer looked welcoming.

'What is it?' asked Jed, looking around the room in fear.

'They're spies sent here to stop our plan!' snarled one young woman in a bright pink tracksuit, whose head seemed to rest on her shoulders at a wonky angle.

'Yeah!' shouted a well-built man whose arms were moving in short, stiff movements. 'Spies could ruin everything.'

'I think there's only one thing for it,' said the waiter, stepping out from behind the counter. 'We have to destroy them!'

Chapter 6

In an instant Jed and the others were off their stools and running towards a fire exit.

Jed spotted something sleek and yellow on a table and snatched it up before its owner could do anything. He then kicked open the exit and the five piled out.

A couple of seconds later everyone else in the café burst outside, screaming and yelling.

'RUN!' urged Mr Graham.

Down the street they pelted, the mob close behind, screeching for them to stop.

Jed took a quick look back and saw that the café crowd had swelled, joined by lots of others. What was going on here? Why had ordering a few drinks sent everyone into such a frenzy?

But he didn't have time to work out the answer. He had his life and the lives of his friends to think about.

They turned a corner and found themselves in an alleyway. Racing down it, they saw there was a low wall at the end.

The five of them vaulted over this, a few moments before their pursuers did the same.

'They're gaining on us!' groaned Tariq.

'THEY MUST BE STOPPED!' screeched a voice, uncomfortably close behind.

Jed had never been so scared; the looks on these weird people's faces were ones of pure hatred.

And then the missiles started flying. The mob picked up anything they could find and threw it: rocks, old drinks cans, pieces of mouldy fruit.

These objects whizzed past Jed and his companions, the occasional item making a direct hit. Luckily nothing was hard enough or powerful enough to inflict any injuries.

On they ran, stumbling over stones and discarded pieces of wood. They entered a small service road. Past trashcans and road-sweeping vehicles they raced, their legs getting heavier by the moment.

'WE'RE NEARLY ON THEM!' barked someone in the crowd.

And they were.

'They're going to get us!' shouted Carla in terror.

'Speed up!' hissed Jed. 'We can't let them get us.'

The five increased their speed, their muscles and joints pulling and hurting. But the crowd sped up too, and now only a few metres separated the two parties.

Up ahead was a very sharp corner. The five runners sped around it and a split-second later a voice hissed at them and ushered them through a narrow, blue door.

Chapter 7

Jed and his party were in a very dark corridor. They listened as the mob ran past outside, their cries muffled and distorted.

A light came on and there in front of them stood Dr Sark.

'I'm so sorry you had to go through that,' he said quietly. 'Some of the people in this town are utter brutes.'

'We ordered some cold drinks and they went crazy,' said Jodie, shaking with fear. 'I don't understand.'

'That's the trouble here,' said Dr Sark. 'The locals don't like anything or anyone that's different from them.

'But you're safe now. They'll burn off all of that hateful energy and later, when the sun has gone down, I'll escort you out of town.'

'How do we know we can trust you?' asked Jed, suddenly suspicious.

'I saved you, didn't I?' said Dr Sark.

'He's right,' said Carla, giving Jed a supportive smile.

The doctor led them along the corridor and then down several others. Each corridor had lots of doors on either side, each door with a frosted glass front.

'Where are you taking us?' asked Mr Graham.

'I reckon the further away you are from that mob the better,' replied the doctor. 'We're nearly there.'

A pocket of unease stirred inside Jed.

If Dr Sark was going to get them out of town when it was dark, why were they going so far into this building? Surely they needed to stay near an exit so that they could make their move quickly?

Jed looked up and saw a sign on the wall:

**FOR EMERGENCIES ONLY:
CALL 769.**

'Here we are,' said the doctor a short while later, pulling a key out of his pocket.

He unlocked a large metal door that led into a tall, rectangular whitewashed room. At the far end was a giant glass window that looked into another, smaller room.

The smaller room was crammed with what looked like large glittering black boxes, housing hundreds of green and red dials.

'Good,' smiled the doctor. 'This is a strong room. There's absolutely no way anyone can get in here. It's the safest place in town.'

'Thank you,' smiled Mr Graham. 'We really appreciate this.'

'It's my pleasure,' said the doctor. 'I have to go and see to a couple of things now, but I'll be seeing you again very shortly.'

He left the room and they heard him lock the door behind him.

'Why'd he lock us in?' asked Tariq.

'He said he'd see us again soon. I'm sure it's fine,' said Jodie, trying to sound reassuring, but not feeling it.

She was right. Just as she said that, Dr Sark appeared on the other side of the glass window.

But this time, instead of behaving normally, his body was making a series of bizarre, jerky movements.

Then suddenly he reached up to his face and, in one jerking movement, pulled off his human face.

Beneath it was the face of a hideous orange-skinned alien.

CHAPTER 8

'NO!!!' yelled Jed, running towards the viewing glass and banging on it with his fists.

The other four hadn't moved. Their fear was freezing them to the spot.

'What a bonus that you five dropped into town,' laughed the new, orange Dr Sark, cruelly. His skin was oily and he had narrow spikes jutting out of his cheeks. His three eyes stared at his five prisoners. It was as if he had no eyelids.

'Who are you?' mouthed Mr Graham in terror.

'Who *we* are is irrelevant to you,' snarled the doctor. 'All you need to know is that, very shortly, I and my kind will be invading Earth, destroying your race and taking over the planet for ourselves!'

'No way!' gasped Jodie.

'Yes way!' snapped the doctor. 'And you gave yourselves away by asking for cold drinks. *We* only drink boiling hot liquids.'

'Is that how you're planning to do it?' asked Jed, his bruised fists still curled into balls.

'You've made yourselves look like us, so no one notices your arrival?'

'Got it in one,' smiled the doctor with glee. 'But as you must have seen by some of our strange body movements, we haven't got it completely right. *Yet.*'

Jed thought about the kids throwing the ball with their stiff movements, the lack of sweat on the mayor's face and the bizarre events taking place in the sports hall.

'You won't get far!' he shouted defiantly. 'We've got armies and air forces that will smash you to pieces!'

'Don't even think it,' replied the doctor. 'Our spacecraft and weapons are far superior to yours. It will all be over in a couple of your Earth hours.'

'Well if that's the case, why don't you let us go?' asked Mr Graham. 'If you're going to destroy all of us, you may as well let us return home to say goodbye to our families and friends.'

'Yes, that would be rather lovely for you. But now that you are here – five REAL humans – I would be a fool to let you go.'

'You saved us from that mob,' pointed out Tariq.

'They would have just ripped you to pieces,' said Dr Sark. 'I would like to take you apart bit by bit. More slowly and much more carefully.'

Jed and the others gulped.

'I have read books of course, but I have never had the chance to investigate the inner workings of the human body properly. Well, today is my lucky day.

'We aren't ready to take over your Earth yet. We need more time. We need to carry out more research. You will help speed things up.'

The 'doctor' opened a cupboard on the wall that was packed with silver medical equipment.

'I think it's time for my investigation to begin!' he chuckled.

CHAPTER 9

'Before you start on us,' said Jed, with terrified wide eyes, 'can you first tell us where on Earth we are?'

'We're not on Earth,' grinned Sark. 'At least not on *your* Earth.'

'What do you mean?' asked Mr Graham.

'We built our own 'Earth' so we could get used to your climate and land formations before we set off,' replied Sark.

'Think of it as a real-world computer model. We call it Earth 2.'

'Instead of taking over Earth, why don't you work together with humans?' said Carla, desperately. 'You could get our Earth and Earth 2 to work together.'

'Do you think I'm an IDIOT?' shouted Sark. 'Your Earth has far more resources than ours. We want your land, your food and your water.

'You see, we use water to power our machines, our spacecraft – and we've noticed you have rather a lot of it!

'Nothing you can do will stop us.'

As Sark was talking, Jed furtively pulled out the sleek yellow object he'd stolen from the café.

It was some kind of mobile phone.

He dialled 769 – the emergency number he'd seen on the wall. Immediately, they could all hear a telephone ringing. It sounded like it was ringing from some distance away.

'Not now!' hissed Dr Sark to himself.

He looked at his captive humans.

'I have to take this call,' he snapped. 'I will be back shortly.'

He hurried out of the room and his oily footsteps echoed and faded as he half-walked, half-slithered, along the corridor.

The others turned to Jed and saw him holding the yellow mobile.

'I think you've just qualified as a genius,' gasped Jodie.

Jed quickly started scanning through the phone's functions. It was obviously more advanced than the kind of smartphones that humans used.

Jed stopped when he came to the *Laser Saw* application. Tapping on this, a pin-point of bright light appeared on the side of the phone.

Jed ran to the door and, to his delight, when he tapped the phone again, a laser beam started cutting a hole right through the door.

A minute later he'd made a space big enough for them each to get through.

Somewhere down the corridors they could hear Dr Sark shouting something.

'Let's go,' said Tariq.

'You go on. I'll catch you up,' whispered Jed.

'Are you crazy?' said Jodie.

'No, just go.'

The others stared at him for a few more seconds and then started running.

Jed stepped over to the door of the smaller room and held up the phone.

A couple of minutes later, he caught up with the others. They were standing in a corridor looking horrified.

Because, standing in front of them and blocking their way, was Dr Sark.

CHAPTER 10

Anger rose up in Jed and he sped towards Sark, leaping into the air as he got nearer.

As he crashed forwards he kicked out his right leg and his right foot made a powerful connection with Sark's repulsive orange head. The blow knocked Sark off his feet and he fell to the ground, unconscious.

Without wasting a second, the five of them reached an exit and ran outside. The mob were at the other end of the street and they immediately turned round.

'IT'S THEM!' yelled someone.

'This way,' said Mr Graham, running in the opposite direction.

The mob screamed and gave chase.

'Where are we going?' panted Carla, as once more they ran for their lives.

'To the Transport Hub I saw on the mayor's map,' replied Mr Graham.

And sure enough, a couple of minutes later they reached a large stretch of open land – a home to about fifty black spaceships.

'WE MUST STOP THEM!' roared the crowd, hot on their heels.

The door to the third spaceship was open and Mr Graham led them all inside. Jed immediately closed and locked the door.

Seconds later, hundreds of furious alien fists were pounding on the door.

Mr Graham and Jodie scanned the control desk. Jodie spotted an AUTO PILOT function.

'There's a pre-programmed route to our planet Earth!' she shouted.

'Activate it immediately!' instructed Mr Graham.

There were now aliens climbing up the sides of the ship, but when Jodie hit the button the ship suddenly shot into the air

with a loud clanking sound. The aliens clinging on were torpedoed back to the ground.

'YES!' shouted Carla, punching the air.

'Look,' said Tariq, 'there's also a *Destroy Earth 2* function here. They're planning to blow Earth 2 up when they've finished with it!'

'Well, as they haven't finished with it yet, why don't we blow it up now and smash all of those aliens to smithereens?' suggested Carla.

'No!' insisted Jed. 'That would make us as bad as them.'

'Jed's right,' nodded Mr Graham. 'You heard what Sark said. They're not ready to take over our Earth yet. Let's destroy Earth 2, but put the destruction on a twelve hour timer.'

'So they can have time to return to their own planet before Earth 2 is wiped out?' asked Tariq.

Mr Graham nodded.

'Maybe when they get home they'll learn to be satisfied with what they've got on their own planet,' said Carla.

'And by us sparing their lives, they might learn to be more tolerant towards others,' added Jed.

Mr Graham pressed the timer and the ship immediately began broadcasting warnings for the aliens to leave Earth 2 and return home.

These warnings continued for five minutes and then the ship left Earth 2's atmosphere and started the journey back to the real Earth.

'What's the first thing you're going to do when you get home?' asked Jodie.

'You know, I could really do with a cold drink,' replied Jed, as Earth 2 receded into the background and the spaceship soared into hyperspace.

More great Toxic reads

Action-packed adventure stories featuring jungles, swamps, deserted islands, robots, space travel, zombies, computer viruses and monsters from the deep.

How many have you read?

JONNY ZUCKER

The Battle of the Undersea Kingdom

by Jonny Zucker

When the local mayor is kidnapped, the people suspect other villages of taking him. But Danny's dad, Tyler, knows more. He thinks that creatures from under the sea are to blame – and he's going to prove it!

75

MORE GREAT TOXIC READS

FOOTBALL FORCE

by Jonny Zucker

It's 2066 and football has changed. Players now wear lightweight body armour. Logan Smith wants to play for the best local team – Vestige United. Their players are fantastic, but Logan suspects that the team has a dark secret.

ISLAND SHOCK

by Jonny Zucker

Mike Chen wakes up on a deserted beach. The last thing he remembers is waiting for a flight at the airport. How did he get here? Where are his friends? Mike soon realises that he is surrounded by danger on all sides. Can he survive the attacks of wild creatures and find out what is going on?

MORE GREAT TOXIC READS

GLADIATOR REVIVAL

by Jonny Zucker

Nick and Kat are on holiday in Rome with their parents. So how do they end up facing the perils of the Coliseum in ancient Rome – as gladiators? Is somebody making a film? Or is this for real and they are fighting for their lives?

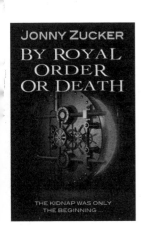

BY ROYAL ORDER OR DEATH

by Jonny Zucker

Miles is a member of the Royal Protection Hub, whose job is to protect the Royal family. When Princess Helena is kidnapped, Miles uncovers a cunning and dangerous plot. Miles must use all his skills to outwit the kidnappers and save the princess's life.

MORE GREAT TOXIC READS

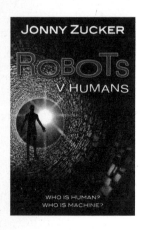

JONNY ZUCKER

ROBOTS V HUMANS

by Jonny Zucker

Nico finds himself with five other kids – all his age. None of them can remember anything from their past. Then they are told that three of them are human and the other three are robots. Can Nico find out who is human and who are the robots?

JONNY ZUCKER

ZOMBIE CAMP

by Jonny Zucker

Arjun and Kev are at summer camp. It's great – there's lots to do and places to explore. But after a while Arjun and Kev begin to suspect that nothing is quite as it seems. Can they avoid the terrible fate that awaits them?

MORE GREAT TOXIC READS

VIRUS 21

by Jonny Zucker

A new computer virus is rapidly spreading throughout the world. It is infecting everything, closing down hospitals, airports and even the internet. Can Troy and Macy find the hackers before the whole world shuts down?

TERROR OF THE SWAMP

by John Townsend

Ex-SAS explorer Baron and his son Greg have been sent to the African jungle to find a lost TV crew. It's a search that brings them face to face with the mysterious ancient terrors of the swamp – and it could cost them their lives.

Jonny Zucker has been a teacher, musician, stand-up comedian and footballer, but now he is best known as one of the most popular authors for children. So far he has written over 100 books.

Jonny also plays in a band and has done over 60 gigs as a stand-up comedian, reaching the London Region Final of the BBC New Comedy awards.

He still dreams of being a professional footballer.